The BIG MONSTER snoReYBOOK

LEIGH HODGKINSON

SPECIAL DELIVERY

Little Monster

nosy crow

Oh dear. I am sorry to say that
you happen to be reading
a **very** dull book.

There is **NOTHING** to see here.
That's right . . .

. . . **NOTHING.**

Little monster

How To Use
OPLAY
OSTOP
ORECORD
HAVE FUN!

Testing, testing, 1, 2, 3.

You see, everyone is fast asleep.

(This is a snoreybook, after all.)

But it's **completely** up to you
if you want to carry on reading . . .

. . . oh good, you have decided to give it a go then, have you?

Well, this is **Norris.**

Unfortunately, Norris fell asleep as soon as you opened this book. Norris's knobbly knees knock while his tiny toothypegs chillily chatter.

Apart from that, there is **NOTHING** to see here.

JIBBER JaBBer

ZZZZZZZZZZZzzz

Before you opened this book,

I DO believe they were talking about YOU.

It's a shame you weren't reading this page then.

Never mind.

Apart from that, there is **NOTHING** to see here.

Here's **TONY.**

Tony's toes tippy tap while he dreams.

Perhaps tomorrow Tony might get around to snipping those terribly tatty toenails.

This here is **FIONa.**

Fiona fussily fidgets and scritches and scratches.

Look, Fiona's five, fluffy, flapping feet are twizzled up into a knot.

If only you'd looked at this page a moment ago – you'd have seen Fiona **frantically** flip onto her back.

Ooh! I think this will be VERY useful.

THUD

THUMP

THUNK

ZZZZZ

ZZ ZZZZ ZZZ

But you missed it, didn't you?
Apart from that, there is
NOTHING to see here.

SCRITCH

SCRATCH

Last of all it's **BRIAN.**

Brian has a super-sized sweet tooth. Brian's **BIG** belly burbles as he dreams of **monster** cream cakes.

If you happen to be **very** sweet, best make sure you are **nowhere** near Brian when he wakes up.

So, that's it – all the snorey monsters in this book. All most DEFINITELY asleep.

Hang about . . .

perhaps I was **wrong**

about this book!

Perhaps there **is**

something going on . . .

Digging holes sure is tiring.

What a noisy alarm clock!

Now those **BIG** monsters

are all wide awake.

And after their monster size snooze

they are ALL VERY hungry . . .

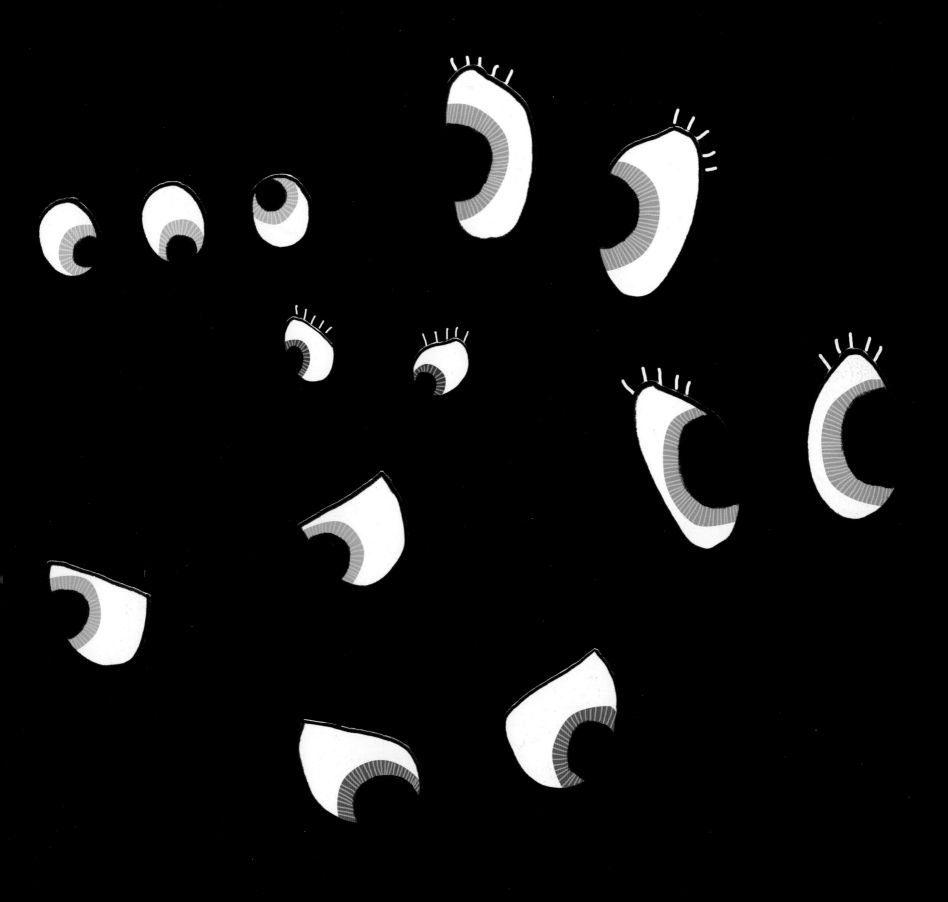

Luckily for you, BIG monsters don't like eating little children.

BIG monsters like eating little **monsters.** You didn't spot a little **monster**, did you?

chitter

JIBBER JABBER

TIPPY

THUD

THUMP **THUNK**

RUMBLY

GRUMBLY

Chatter

BIBBLE BaBBle

TAP TAP

SCRITCH SCRatch SCRITCH

GROWL

What's all that NOISE? It couldn't be an even BIGGER monster, could it? What do you suppose an even BIGGER monster might like to eat?

Well, these BIG monsters sure aren't going to stick around to find out!

Hee hee! I LOVE it when a plan comes together!

Well, that's got rid of all those
BIG noisy monsters.

Let's all enjoy a little bit

of peace and quiet now, shall we?

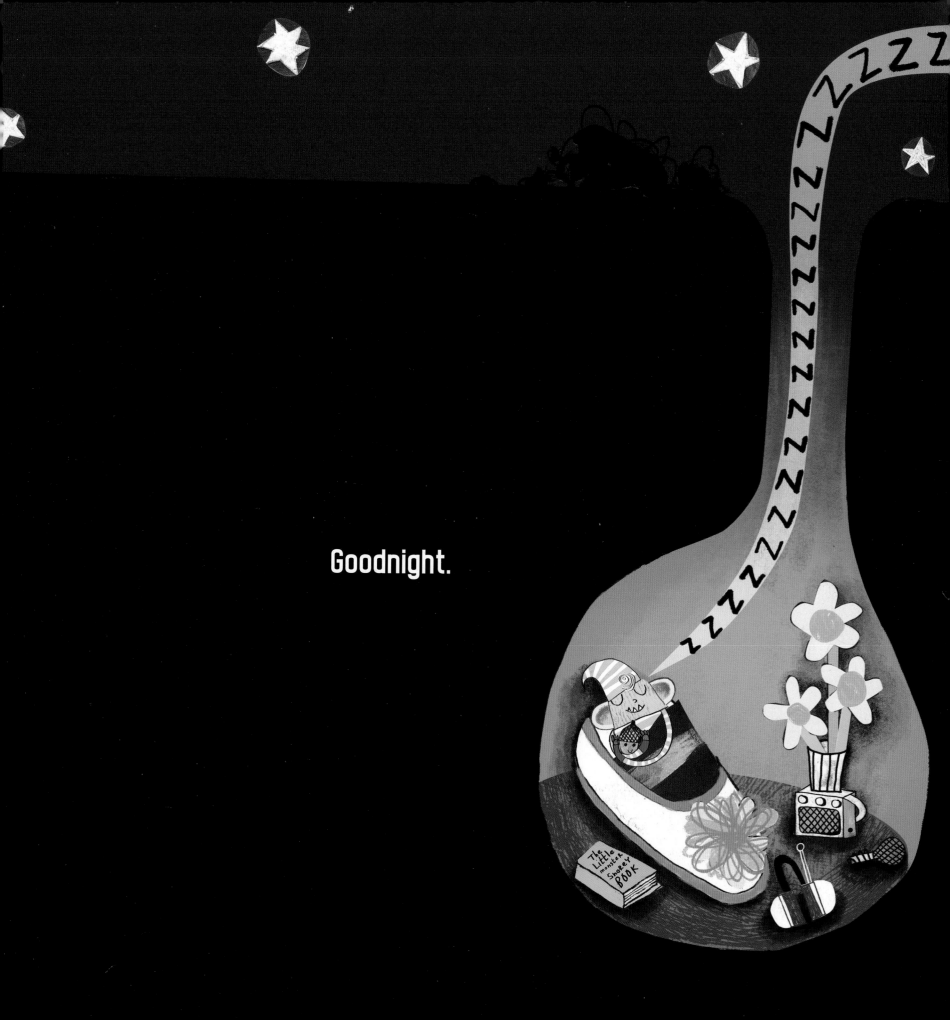

Goodnight.